Grandma's Garden

Ruth Thomson
Illustrated by Evie Safarewicz

Family Learning

My grandma does not need to shop.

She grows her food instead.

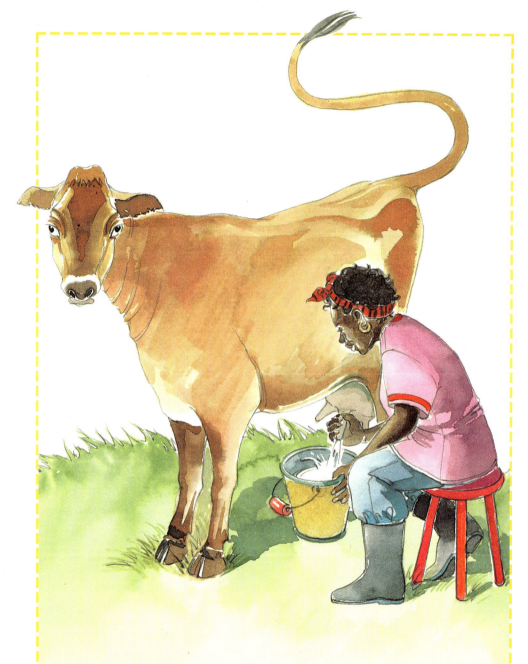

She has a cow to give her milk,

and makes her own good bread.

Her big brown hens lay
big brown eggs.

She picks apples from her trees.

Her cabbages all grow in rows.

Her honey comes from bees.

In Grandma's garden lots of things are big and fat and tall.

It's fun to help her grow her food.
I like to eat it best of all.

In the spring, we dig the ground

and sow long rows of seeds.

And then we have to water well

and pull up all the weeds.

In the summer, string beans grow,

as well as sweet green peas.

The strawberries are red and ripe.

May I have some, please?

On windy days in early fall,

we make sweet apple pies.

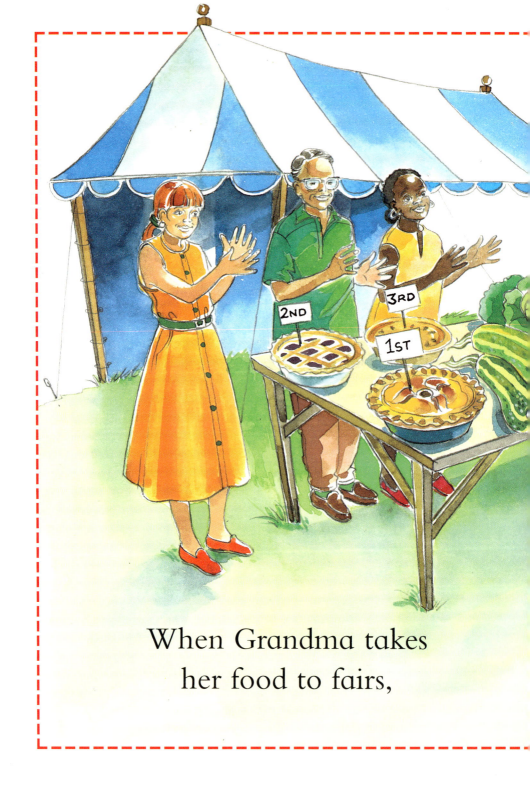

When Grandma takes her food to fairs,

she always wins first prize.

Picture Words

Grandma   milk   bread

eggs   apple trees

cabbages   honey   bees

seeds   string beans   peas

strawberries   pie